Soul Fire

Elle Klass

Soul Fire

Copyright©2023 by Elle Klass
Published by Books by Elle, Inc.
ISBN: 978-1-951017-44-6
All rights reserved
Editor Dawn Lewis
Cover art TL Katt

Author's Disclaimer

Realm Walker

Books in the Realm Walker Series
In the Shadows
The Land of Lost Souls
Hidden Passages
The Ring of Betrayal

Realm Walker Prequel
Heart of Darkness
Soul of Malice

Other Realm Walker Companion Books
The Origin: Marya's Journal
Soul Fire

Realm Walker World Books – coming soon!
Love at Frost Bite
Accidental Ghost: Soul Catcher Vol.1

Other Young Adults Series
The Bloodseeker
Zombie Girl
Hidden Journals
Baby Girl

1

Halsey

I'd never felt sillier than in my roommate's commoner denim pants she called jeans. With holes in the thighs and lower legs, I looked like a peasant. That was the purpose of course. I'd borrowed them so I could find a legendary scroll hidden in my realm of Navarin.

When I say *my* realm I mean it literally, as I'm the Diama who will one day be queen. I couldn't go prancing around with a common sky fae and bringing attention to myself while searching for a grimoire that contained a level 4 magic spell that used sacrifice to modify realms and turn everyday hybrids into creatures with magnificent power. A grimoire that was said to possibly exist, but no one had ever seen it.

What had I gotten myself into? I shifted the floppy hat out of my eyes as I read the words on the page of the mysterious book we found. No. Terra, my roommate found the ancient text that would lead us to Merla's grimoire. Merla was a powerful and tricky sea fae. Terra wouldn't have found it on her own. My part was crucial as I provided the transportation and wet suits to go deep into the lavender sea and find Merla's cave. It was a perk of being the Diama.

"What does it say or hand it over? You asked me to help," Bjorn, my annoying partner, demanded. His green hair more the color of spring than the sand beneath our feet. Matching green freckles bounced on his cheeks.

"Be patient!" I wouldn't have even asked him, except Terra insisted he join us on our excursion to the bottom of the lavender sea, along with her *other* fae friend. A sea fae, except they were both gone on a covert mission. She hadn't filled me in on the details. "In the cavern beneath Mer Point you find the fairy dust of Ansley, a mighty and tricky land fae with impeccable skill."

"You know, if you'd share the book with me I could read it on my own. I'm not royalty, but I'm not illiterate, and read old fae as well as you," he said shaking his head and rolling his eyes. "C'mon. I'm sure the precious Diama has no idea how to get below Mer Point."

Whatever! "Because this has to stay secret doesn't mean you can treat me as a common fae. I won't forget this excursion when I'm queen," I barked with pointed words.

His lips twisted into a smile. "I'm sure you won't, and neither will I. It won't look good if I accidently let it slip."

He was infuriating! He wouldn't, would he? The look on his smug face said he would. Who would believe him over the queen?

"Are you going to stand there or are we going to find some powerful land fae dust?" he called as he walked to the shore.

Navarin was covered in the lavender seas. Islands made up small landmasses where most fae lived. Each island made of light green sand, and fairy dust sparkled everywhere. It was the dust of the dead. When a fae dies their life is celebrated and they fade into dust that reaches every crevice of Navarin.

I climbed into the small two-person boat after him. It was barely large enough for two people and the hard bench wasn't comfortable beneath me. This would be so much easier if I didn't have to do it in secret.

"Mevan," he said, dropping dust into the water and the boat scooted off the shore. He grabbed an oar and handed it to me.

I brought my hands up. "No, I don't row boats."

Throwing it at me, it hit my thigh. "I'm not your servant and I can't row this thing straight. It needs two people rowing to move in a straight line. That's how it works. We row together and guide it." Narrowing his eyes he snapped, "You know there are fae who do this for fun and sport?"

"I'm not one of them. Why don't we use magic?" I dipped my hand into the water as I said, "Akipe Mer Point."

He rocked the boat, causing me to clutch the sides tightly.

"You afraid of the sea?" he teased as he let go of the sides of the small water vessel.

"No. Why are you so mean?"

He raised his hands in the air. "It was a joke."

"It wasn't funny. Stop being…being…so you!"

He leaned back against the curved arch of the small boat behind him and kicked his legs over the side. "It seems you've got this all figured out."

My contempt for him reached new levels. *I hated him!*

2

Bjorn

Halsey was beautiful and radiated a glow of superiority. I wasn't about to admit anything to the spoiled fae. She was the epitome of what most fae tried not be; a conceited, high and mighty, unpleasant, entitled brat.

The short tips of her ears poked above the graceful waves of her blonde hair and her blue eyes blinked as if expecting me to do everything like everyone had done all her life. Her servants had servants. I kicked my feet up, put my arms behind my head and relaxed. Let her use magic to steer the tiny kayak. It wasn't a bother to me.

Soul Fire

She'd never lifted a finger. This grimoire hunt was more to prove something to herself than anyone else, especially her roommate Terra. They were on opposite sides of the pendulum. When one swung upwards the other downwards. It would be worth the weight of all the precious stones of Verboten to see how those two tolerated each other in the confines of their dorm.

I was along for the ride and laughs. If she really wanted to find the grimoire which didn't exist. It was legend. There was never any proof such a powerful object existed in Navarin or any other realm. It was something people whispered about behind closed doors. Level 4 magic was the most powerful magic there was and it didn't come free. To use it took blood and sacrifice, so the legend said. If she wanted the grimoire, she'd have to be an active team player, suck up her royal pride, and get dirty like the common folk.

Her eyes shifted to the open sea as the small kayak moved through the low waves and into the open sea. Slender curves shone in her roommate's clothing. It fit tighter than her own. I studied her shapely form as my eyes moved from her legs, over her chest, stopping for a moment as her chest heaved, then up to her chin. She was the most physically desirable fae, yet her personality didn't merely kill the mood it squashed and ground it to a pulp.

Realm Walker

Soft-styled blonde waves fell against the sides of her cheeks as she pushed the silly hat further on her head after a wind gust nearly knocked it off. She was embarrassed to be seen with a sylph and doing something her royal butt would be in deep trouble for. Not that I thought she'd ever face any real consequences for her actions.

On the other hand, if my parents knew what I was up to I'd have a lot of explaining to do after their lecture. That was the real punishment. As sky fae, they weren't in holy worship of the crown and would despise me spending time with the Diama. She hadn't glanced my way as I studied every curve and valley of her. Halsey hadn't a clue that the realm lacked respect for the crown. Monarchies were outdated.

The wind kicked up and she pressed her hand to the hat in order to keep it on her head. The boat rocked in the choppy waves. She turned her head, wild eyes meeting my gaze. "Stop it! I mean it!"

"We're in the sea, there's waves. It's a thing that happens," I snarled, lowering my leg and kicking an oar at her.

She pulled her hand back as if the oar had spikes and teeth and held on as a wave carried us high enough to see the ledge of Mer Point straight ahead. A green tail splashed into the water and dove under the kayak. I lost sight as the kayak dropped.

Soul Fire

Her fingers clutched around the sides so hard blood rushed to her knuckles. "Better start rowing. Kayaks are meant for two."

Stiff as a sheet dried in the sun and speechless, she pushed her back straight and screamed as the kayak lifted then dropped, water splashing over the sides. Another wave pushed us up and forward. As we fell, the kayak rolled to the side and we plunged into the sea.

Through the sparkles and dust I saw her bewildered eyes as she waved her arms in distress. I pushed towards her, the water moving between my arms. Green scales flashed beneath her as a Mer shoved her upward with its strong tail.

I caught her hand and we floated upward. She spat water out of her mouth as we crawled in the sand towards the shore of the picturesque island.

3

Halsey

I spat sand out of my mouth as I crawled onto the small beach area on the other side of the island from Mer Point. My magic hadn't worked so good, or the sea wasn't as amiable as I hoped. Not that I was admitting that to Bjorn.

"Take my hand," he offered in a soft voice. I did, with hesitation. He explained with a mocking tone, "Magic is wonderful and Navarin is full of it but the sea has its own ideas and all the dead sea fae and their dust don't always do what you want. Even for a future queen. I'm sorry you had to learn the hard way."

Ignoring his bad attitude, I climbed to my feet and let go of his hand. "Let's find this dust and get out of here." I reached down and grabbed the soggy hat, shaking the sand off it.

We hiked to the other side of the island and passed a small group of fae. I turned my head away from them. Bjorn waved and took a step towards them. I grabbed his arm. "What are you doing? You can't approach them."

"Sure I can. Watch!"

I dropped my arm from his. If it was possible to hate him more, I did. Holding my hat in place as a sea breeze rushed over me, I stared up the hilly path to Mer Point.

"If you're going to pose as a common fae you need to act like one," he said upon his return. "Those fae know the island. If we want to get below Mer Point we need to swim beneath it. There's an entrance to a cavern. It's never visible, even during low tide."

"Did you tell them what we are looking for?"

He shot an angry glance my way. "You think that? I don't like you. You're annoying and think you're better than everyone else, but I'm not about to jeopardize both of us by telling someone what we are doing. Don't underestimate me because I didn't grow up in the white palace." He turned away from me and marched around the hill that would take us to the point.

His words scorched as they bit. Was that what he thought? I ran to close the distance between us. "I'm not easy. I'm spoiled and I'll be the queen one day, and I don't like you much either, but I also have feelings. That's why I'm here. I've never liked Terra," – my roommate at the academy – "except she's grown on me and she's right and…" I squeezed my hands together because I hated to even admit it. "You're right. I don't know what it is to be common, average."

He stopped and faced me. "I get that. That's why I'm here. I like Terra too."

I lowered my eyebrows and blinked away the tears starting to form. I'd been honest with him, pleaded my heart, and he *liked Terra too*. He hated me!

"Don't get so wimpy-eyed and emotional. You're not so bad if you'd stop being so… you."

I bit my lip and blinked hard. The first tear rolled down my cheek.

"I don't like you. We'll never be friends but we can work together." He met my eyes with a goofy expression on his face. His eyes wide, nose scrunched, and lips twisted into a halfhearted smile.

I nodded and dried up my tears.

We came around the island. Water splashed hard along the wall that extended to

Soul Fire

Mer Point. It shadowed the small beach area beneath it that was more or less, depending on the tide, but never more than enough for two people to stand on.

I couldn't see a thing from the slice of beach. It looked like rocks. Relentless waves splashed against them. "Are you sure?"

"One way to find out." He pulled his shirt off, revealing a muscle-toned chest. It caught my eye and I immediately looked away. He was the kid who zoomed around Provence Academy on his glider. From the corner of my eye, as I couldn't pull them completely away, I noted him strip his shoes off and dive in.

"What are you doing?"

His head bobbed above the water for a moment, long enough to say: "Finding the cavern."

I wanted to scream as I stamped my feet. Throwing a tantrum wouldn't change anything. I didn't know whether to wait or dive in. Several minutes went by and I was ready to pull my hat and shoes off to go in when he reappeared.

"Found it. Jump in and stay with me."

Taking a deep breath, I tossed my hat and shoes off and jumped in after him. The water in Navarin was always warm and felt nice against my skin. The sea was clear except for the fairy dust, but it sparkled in the higher depths. It was dark as I followed him down and I couldn't help being a little nervous when I could barely make out his feet in front of me. Then they vanished and hands wrapped around my waist pulling me upward.

I let off a scream in the water as the hands pulled me down and let go. My head bobbed upward and met Bjorn's face above the surface of the water. "What was that about?" I asked.

"I didn't want you to swim over it. It docs get dark, even with the dust. There isn't enough light. There it is."

The cave was beneath Mer Point. Sea water splashed against the rocky wall and further in was a sandy spit.

Crawling onto the small spit, I pulled the book out. The book was magic and water repellent, so I hadn't worried. I opened it up to the page I'd marked to see if anything else appeared. A drawing formed in front of my eyes.

"It appears as we go," Bjorn said from behind me, glancing at the book over my shoulder.

I twisted around and pulled the book towards me. "Yes, now back away."

"Partners, remember. We work together."

"Fine." I laid the book in the sand.

He stared at it for a minute and raised his head. "Over there. Look, it's that wall."

He pointed toward the wall furthest from the entrance. "We're here, so it's there."

The drawing was the inside of the cave, focusing on the one wall. I brought the book with me as we stood in front of it. "What do we do now?" I asked.

He leaned in and looked at the drawing again and pointed. "Something is written on the wall."

"No, there isn't." I glanced back at the picture and, sure enough, words were scrolled across on it in old fae. It was the language of our ancestors, but all fae learned it as we used it for magic. We read the words together and the wall disappeared. Inside was a long-packed sand bed filled with dust.

"I think we found Ansley," Bjorn remarked.

4

Halsey

We collected the dust in a small container that Bjorn put in his pocket. My roommate Terra was a bit smaller than me around the hips and her pants were too tight to fit the container of dust and my bra would be holding the book. We both looked at the book as words appeared on the next page. *Deep in the mangroves opposite the white palace you will find the dryad. She must give you a leaf willingly. One stolen will stop you in your tracks.*

I shuddered at the words. I had no intention of stealing anything from anyone. "What is a dryad?"

"I guess we're about to find out."

Tonight? It was getting late. "We should head back to the school and meet back tomorrow."

"No, we don't have classes tomorrow. Are you afraid?" he asked with a challenging expression on his face. An eyebrow raised, one side of his lips higher than the other.

Was my fear and uncertainty that obvious? "I'm scared. It's late and dark and we don't know what a dryad is. We don't even have a boat to get us there."

He pondered my words for a minute then licked his lips. "I got it! We don't need a boat. I can fly."

I closed my eyes and let out an aggravated breath. "But I can't."

"You don't need to. I'm strong enough to carry you on my back as I fly."

He was a sky fae with a well-developed chest. I hadn't studied his back, but if it looked anything like his chest then he probably could carry me. He wasn't a small fae, nearly a foot taller than me…*What am I thinking even considering it?*

One look into his lavender eyes and it was my only choice. I followed him back to the smaller slice of shoreline. My shirt and hat were dry but not for long since I was soaked. I rung out my short blonde hair and slipped the hat over my head.

"You know we'll be flying. There's lots of wind."

"And?"

He laughed. "That hat won't stay on your head."

I hadn't thought of that. Dropping my eyes to cover my embarrassment I took the hat off. "Fine, I'll hold onto it for later."

"Yeah," he mumbled with an eye roll.

He decided the best place to take off was Mer Point and so we made the hike up the hilly path. The water splashed hard and sank down, then did it again. It was hard to believe we'd just been down there.

"Climb on my back and wrap your legs around me."

"Try not to enjoy yourself," I snapped, trying to hide my pout as I pulled myself onto his bare back. His skin was soft under my fingers. Tiny bits of sand collected between my hands and him. The hat held in my right hand, I wrapped my legs around his waist, and wings grew from his sides. They were the same green as his freckles and hair. I didn't realize how thick fae wings were. He was part dragon. That could add thickness to them. They were feathered like fae wings.

His chuckle caused me to slip on his back. "I'll try not to, Diama."

Errr! Why was he so irritating? I inhaled deep and ignored his comment as his wings flapped against his side, pushing the air down as we rose.

The job of the sky fae was to confuse the enemy with their colors. I felt a little confused now watching his majestic feathers flap and ohhh… My stomach fell as we dropped off the point and almost hit the water below then soared into the sky. I wanted to kick him for scaring me. I was sure he'd done that on purpose. Instead, I closed my eyes.

Air rushed beneath us, the hat flapped back against his bare chest and we seemed to level out. Opening my eyes slowly, the sight was amazing. I could see so much of the realm. The islands seemed smaller above than on them and the sea went on endlessly. It sparkled with bioluminescent organisms and fairy dust.

I tightened my legs around him and slid my arms down his chest. I was practically hugging him. The muscles in his back tightened and moved with his wings as they rubbed against my breasts. I laid my head against his shoulders.

A series of lights came in to view as we soared downward. I blinked and lifted my head when I realized what they were. The white palace. I recognized the spires. My home. It looked so different and not as large from the air. We coasted over it and tilted. I tightened my legs more to keep from sliding.

"Go with it!" he hollered into the air. The sound vibrated against my ear drums.

Was I squeezing him? I loosened my feet a little and realized they were lower than his waist and a hair above…somewhere I didn't want them to be.

"Hold on but don't dig your heels in," he said as we soared downward at a fast speed.

I couldn't hold in my scream as it looked like we were going to crash into a bunch of trees. Squeezing my eyes shut, I expected the trees to shred my arms. He stopped and water splashed.

"I know you can't resist my charm and good looks but we're here."

I opened my eyes. His feet were standing in the water of the mangrove. I climbed off and situated my clothing as my shirt had come up exposing my abdomen. "We are. How do we find the dryad? It's dark."

"We're fae," he responded in a questioning tone. Mixing the dust in the air, he said the old fae word for light and all the dust in the trees and floating in the air sparkled.

"I thought the magic does its own thing. How did that work for you?"

"I asked nicely."

So had I. He was infuriating! All my life the dust always worked for me and never gave me a problem. "You! You capsized the boat, didn't you? So you'd get me to ride on you as we flew over Navarin. Right! A common fae escorting the Diama." I pressed my hand against my head. *How did it take me this long to figure it out?*

"There you go. Life is all about Halsey. You," he pointed a finger at me, "did the spell that capsized the boat. I think you enjoyed our little flight so much you feel guilty." He pushed out his bare, muscled chest.

I visibly shuddered in anger and followed the string of lit dust. It was my turn to leave him behind, anger unceremoniously billowing from my ears and nose. Maybe it was a mistake to bring him along in the first place. I could do this on my own. I didn't need him or anyone! Water splashed over my legs to my thighs as I traipsed through the water, forgetting I was alone in the mangroves; a place no fae goes. When the leaves of the trees started moving low and the water spread in small waves around my legs and a foul smell accosted my nose, I stopped.

My eyes grew wide as something broke the surface of the water.

5

Halsey

I reached for the closest branch and pulled my legs up over it. It lowered and I hung just above the water and something broke its surface. In a panic, I scooted towards the middle of the tree. My head hanging upside down, I saw how ugly it was. Its hair spiked and large teeth. I gagged then pulled myself together. I needed a spell. The only thing I could think of was capto for cage but the word didn't come out right. It was more cato which meant rope, only the rope didn't tie him up it landed in the water next to him

Soul Fire

Chuckles filled my ears followed by: "I guess the magic isn't on your side. Did you mean capto?" Bjorn said as he swirled the dust with a finger and pushed it toward the thing in the water. His face so smug I wanted to kick him. "Is that how you hugged me in the air? You're quite flexible for a Diama."

More scared of the thing in the cage, I didn't respond to his goading. "What is that thing?!"

"I don't know," he said, picking up the cage with the ugly, smelly thing in it. It wasn't more than ten to fifteen centimeters in height, with claws on its fingers and barefoot. "Why don't we ask it?"

Ask it? Did it even talk? The fae were a beautiful people, how had that thing been here hiding and nobody knew?

The thing bent down and bowed my direction. "Diama," it said, stressing each syllable.

"It's bowing to you and it talks. What more do you want?" he asked me. It wasn't a question but a sarcastic comment. He refocused on the caged thing and asked, "You aren't fae, so what are you?" Bjorn asked.

I stayed clung to the tree. Moving my arms over the branch so I hung at my elbows.

"Me, Balster of the dark nymph," it said as it rose from its bow.

Dark nymphs. Those were legend not real. It was said they used to inhabit Provence

City before it was Provence City but there were no actual sightings of them ever recorded.

Bjorn continued his discussion with the dark nymph while I hung upside down impatiently in the tree. "Do you know where to find the dryad?"

"Yes, me know, yes." It nodded.

Bjorn tilted his head and looked at me. "What do you say, Diama? You going to get out of that tree?"

No! Yes, it was horribly uncomfortable and the blood was rushing to my head. "Is it safe? Are there more?"

"You Diama," it pointed at me, "we help."

The way it said *we* caused chills to rush up my spine and I lifted my head. Another one stood on a higher branch looking down at me like I was its next meal. Out of shock and fear, I uncurled my legs and dropped into the water. Stumbling backwards, I fell on my hands, the slimy dirt squishing against my palms. I jumped up and screamed pointing a slimy finger towards the tree. "There's more!"

Bjorn stayed calm as I grabbed his free arm with a slimy hand and scooted closer to him. The nymph in the cage stared at me.

Ignoring me, Bjorn talked to it. I stamped my foot, water splashing up to our thighs. "If I let you out, will you take us to the dryad?"

"Yes, we take, dryad."

"No!" He had good hearing but wasn't listening. "In the tree. There's another one."

"You wouldn't hurt the Diama, right?"

It nodded. "Eat, sea serpents. One by her leg. Me protect her."

I jumped. Serpents. This was bad. *Why did I think I could ever do this?* Then think I could do it on my own? Navarin was a scarier and more unfriendly place than I ever realized.

"Not anymore." Bjorn shook his head and looked at it. "You'll keep the snakes away."

"Yes."

He opened the cage and the dark nymph jumped out. The one in the tree leaped from one branch to another until it hit the water and joined the other.

We traipsed through the water for hours it felt like then the dark nymphs ahead stopped. One dipped below the water.

"Stay still and quiet," Bjorn whispered.

I looked to the dirt under the trees as a possible safe refuge. I blinked several times to be sure I was seeing what I thought. "The dirt is moving! Look!" I pointed.

"Do you not understand what quiet means? Stop screaming. You're not only hurting my ears but attracting whatever the nymphs are after."

My body shuddered as something pushed against my leg. I couldn't stop the shaking. The water splashed in front of me as the other dark nymph went under.

"Bjorn! Bjorn!" I jumped towards him and clutched my arms around his neck, scooting my legs as high as I could get them.

He placed his arms under my butt for extra support. "You really can't resist me. I've been told I have that effect on women."

"Don't flatter yourself. I have no interest in you other than you protecting your Diama! Don't think of moving your hands any higher." I snapped and warned. Through the corner of my eye I watched as the water splashed where I was standing and a long thing with a pointy head was thrust over the water's surface and crashed back down, sending ripples into the moving dirt of the shoreline.

Bjorn didn't move and the dark nymphs appeared again, arguing over whose dinner the long thing with the pointy head was. I got a good look at the sea serpent as Balster tore its head off and spat it to the shore line, then ripped it in two and handed part of it to the other nymph.

"I think I'm going to be sick," I mumbled just as the heaving began.

Soul Fire

Bjorn dropped me and I fell back into the water. "Not on me, Diama."

A few heaves later and I was able to stand. It wasn't much further when we finally reached a dead end.

"Dryad here," Balster said as he parked on the moving soil.

6

Halsey

There was nothing but a tree. The branches moved and the trunk wiggled. I stepped back and hid behind Bjorn.

As if stretching from a long slumber, the branches expanded and, in disbelief, I watched an ordinary tree turn into a person with green skin. She didn't look scary. I had this. "Are you the dryad?"

"Who is asking?"

I stepped away from Bjorn and towards her. "I'm the Diama of Navarin and I'm here to collect something very important. I have to ask you for a leaf."

"There are plenty of leaves and plenty of trees. Why do you ask me?"

The book said she must give it willingly, but not that I needed to divulge why. I repeated and specified, "I need one of your leaves."

It put a green hand under its chin as it leaned forward and studied me. "What do I get in exchange?"

I didn't have anything. I wasn't even wearing my own clothes. What did a dryad that hid in the mangroves need that I could give it? "As the Diama, I can offer you peace in the mangroves."

"You don't look like a Diama with your filthy, torn clothes. If you are who you say there is one thing you can give me that won't cost you anything."

That sounded like a deal. 'What is it?"

"I've always wanted to see a unicorn."

No way! I wasn't transforming into a unicorn in front of anyone in the nasty mangroves with moving soil, sea serpents, and dark nymphs! I'd get my white fur all dirty. I stepped back.

"Can I have a minute with her?" Bjorn asked the dryad.

She nodded.

Speaking low, he said, "All she wants is to see a unicorn. Remember the warning. You can't steal it. It must be given and you're a unicorn."

Why was he right?! As a land fae, I could transform into a majestic white unicorn.

I squeezed my eyes and pursed my lips. "Fine!" The two dark nymphs, dryad, and Bjorn were all looking at me, plus anything else I didn't know about that was in the mangrove. "Can you all look away while I transform?"

The group met glances and nodded. This was turning out to be so much work! I loved my unicorn self but it wasn't something we did every day. Our unicorn was symbolic. In ancient times the unicorns were powerful land warriors. Bjorn's eyes watched me under a flap of green hair. I narrowed my gaze at him and he turned to the side.

I harnessed my unicorn and let it out, my legs in the murky water and hooves against the slimy bottom of the mangrove. Involuntarily, I cringed followed by a stutter, "OK, you can turn around."

Bjorn stepped back and pressed a hand on my back. "Wow!"

"Can you make your horn light up?" the dryad asked, as if transforming wasn't enough.

Sure, I could, but hadn't she asked enough already? My white fur was getting dirty and the slime was gathering in my hooves. I rolled my eyes at the look on the dryad and Bjorn's faces and lit my horn.

"It's beautiful," the dryad said, her eyes focused on the light as she shed a leaf.

Soul Fire

Bjorn caught it in his hands and stuffed it in his pocket with the fairy dust. He put an arm under my neck and whispered, "Walk away."

I stepped backwards, my hooves squishing in the slime. The dryad and nymphs stood motionless as if in a trance by my horn. I finally turned my body around to run when Bjorn accosted my neck and slid his legs over my back. *What was he doing?!*

He tapped his feet against my sides, "Run now!"

I didn't understand the hurry and wanted to yell at him to get off my back but I was so anxious to get out of the mangrove I didn't care anymore. Running as fast as I could with an air fae on my back, I forgot about the nasty squishing between my hooves. When we reached the edge of the mangrove I put on the brakes and slid into the mouth of the sea. Bjorn flew over my head, splashing into the lavender sea where it met the mangrove.

"That was awesome!" Sea water over his abs, thighs, and ankles. His hands pressed behind him as he sat up.

"Look away!" I demanded, as I was ready to shift back.

He turned his head as I transformed into my fae self. "What was that about?" I demanded.

Standing, he turned around and faced me, his lavender eyes sparkling under the stars. "Nothing. I've always wanted to ride a unicorn and it seemed like a good time to get out of there."

What?! He made my blood pressure rise. "I hate you!" I screamed as I tackled him, pushing him back into the water. That was it! The final straw. I had officially snapped.

He caught his arms around me and flipped me over, water splashed over my face. His hand snaked behind my neck to hold my head above the water, his body pressed firmly against mine. Our lips brushed.

Quickly, he jumped up as if embarrassed or uncomfortable and stood above me. He shook his hair back and offered me a hand. "I was wrong, but it was amazing. Admit it."

Accepting his hand, heat rising in my cheeks from the awkward intimate moment we shared, I adjusted my clothing and admitted, "It was sort of fun. I don't transform a lot." Panic hit me when I realized the soft cover of the thin book wasn't buried under my bra. "The book!"

7

Halsey

"**Y**ou lost it?!"

"No," I retorted. "I didn't lose it. You made me lose it." Leaning down, I splashed in the water. He stood there, doing nothing. "Are you going to help?"

A corner of his lip edged upward, then the other corner. His hand slipped around his back. "You didn't lose anything. It fell when you transformed, and I caught it."

You couldn't say that from the moment we reached the sea? Stifling my rising anger, I pushed my loathing for him towards my feet. *Breathe, Halsey. Breathe.* At least we had it and didn't need to go back into the mangrove.

He brought the book around to the front of him, opened it and read. "In the ruins of the old palace in the walls you will find a crown that belonged to Queen Giseppa, mother of the elfin."

"The old palace?" It gave me the creeps to even think about it. It was once a thriving metropolis, but after Giseppa (I didn't feel she earned the title queen) left the king and went to Aradia the metropolis fell as he mourned her the rest of the days of his life.

"That's what it says." He leaned down. "Climb on."

What choice did I have? He didn't try anything funny this time and the ride was pleasant. I reveled in the beauty of my realm. The island of the old palace was completely dark as we glided over it. I had a bad feeling but hoped we were almost at the end of our hunt.

He brought us directly to the old palace remains on the hill, most of the island visible from our location. Water lapped at the edges of the shore. Buildings half erect, mostly crumbled as sand. The steps to the castle intact, we stood above them at the entrance. There was no door so we went in. "Does the book show us anything?"

He leaned close to me as he opened it. A picture formed, like in the cavern below Mer Point. It was a map of the castle and footsteps moved through the halls and up the stairs then finally stopped.

We followed them. I hoped the staircase was still there. Not much was left of an old palace made of sand bricks. Around one corner then another. The windows and walls mostly gone; a chilly breeze swept over us. I wrapped my arms around myself to keep in the warmth.

Bjorn noticed and pulled me closer. "We can't have the Diama catch a cold," he said. His bare skin and arm felt good against me, and I didn't fight the gesture.

We arrived at the steps. They were intact, but not the banister. I took Bjorn's hand as he lowered his arm from me and offered it. Staying to the center of the steps, we took them slowly and carefully. Each step I worried would weaken the unstable stairs and send us crashing down. When we reached the final one I felt better, but not for long. There was no wall on either side, or railing, and we were a few meters in the air. He kept his hand around mine as we walked over what was left of the floor.

Bjorn stayed in front of me then stopped. "I hate to be the one, Diama, to tell you this but we're going to have to jump."

I leaned around him and peered down. There was a gap that was at least half a meter, and below were two solid metal thrones. They hadn't been weathered or destroyed over the years, nor had anyone stolen them. They were there and probably made of precious metal. The stars and moonlight twinkled in the stones. They had to be worth a fortune. Probably heavy and hard to steal too. When I got home after this excursion, I'd request the thrones be put in the museum.

"I'll go first. When I get to the other side, all you need to do is jump towards me and I'll catch you."

His words didn't make me feel any better. I brushed the hair out of my eyes as he jumped. Landing on both feet, he fell forward slightly but lifted his hands to the side and steadied himself. He turned and held out his hands. I took a deep breath and released, then again.

"I'm ready. You're going to catch me, right?"

"I may joke, Diama, but not with your life."

Squeezing my eyes shut, one cracked a sliver, I shuddered and nodded then leapt towards him. His arms slid around my back as my feet landed on solid ground. We scooted backwards away from the edge before he finally moved his arms.

"I think you like feeling me against you," I joked snidely to lesson the fear and tension I was feeling.

"You do feel good." He smiled like he meant it. Not the cocky annoying smile, but one that said 'I'm falling for you.' Opening the book again, we looked at the footsteps. They ended in front of us but nothing was there. No wall, nothing.

"That can't be!" I freaked and my mouth ran faster than my brain. Everything rolled off my tongue and I was powerless to stop it. "This whole thing was Terra's idea. She talked me into it! It's all because of her that I'm wet and dirty. I've been wet all day. My hair is a mess. My shoes are ruined. Her clothes are ruined. I had to turn into a unicorn for a leaf! I lost the stupid book. I was almost eaten by a sea serpent or dark nymph and now there's no wall! We'll never find that stupid scroll!"

Bjorn looked at me with a calm face, one eyebrow lifted.

"And why are you always calm?!"

"Are you done?" he asked, holding the folded book against his legs.

I sniffed back the cry and frantic moment. "Yes."

He pressed his hands against my shoulders. The book still in his hand. "Diama. We can do this. We have two items that we need. The book shows us a new one each time we find one and tells us where to go. It's not hard and, yeah, you're probably going to get dirtier and need a long, hot royal shower when you're done, but we can do this."

"Promise?" I sniffled, after his sarcastic pep talk.

He pulled me in and pressed me against him, then brought a hand under my chin and lifted it. "I promise."

I sniffled again and wiped away the tears rolling down my cheek. He was so gentle and patient with me. I was seeing a new side to him. One I liked very much and I enjoyed feeling his body close to mine. "OK."

When he pulled away the sand fell beneath us and we dropped. A scream filled the air, piercing my ears. I realized it was mine. We were going to die!

8

Halsey

Sand shot up around me as I landed in a pile of it. Pushing it away and spitting it out, I unburied myself and found Bjorn. He'd landed about a meter away. Pushing the sand away from him, it slid down the mound we were on top of.

"You promised." I couldn't help the wave of tears. This was it. The last straw. We'd never find the crown under all the sand. It was hopeless.

Bjorn moved closer and pressed his lips against mine. I moved my torso backwards. "What are you doing?"

"Making you be quiet and stop crying."

"I…uh…" The words didn't form, my mind went blank. He did stop me from crying by changing my focus. His soft lips felt right against mine, but I wasn't about to admit that. "How do we find this crown? Does the book show us anything else?"

Both of us waist deep in sand. He pulled the book out of the back of his pants and shook out the sand. "No. The footsteps stopped and there's nothing more. See?"

He showed it to me. We'd come so far, disappointment radiated down my spine, followed by a wave of relief. No grimoire, but we were done and I could shower. "I guess we're done then. This is over and I want to go home and sleep in my bed!"

I slid down the sand hill on my belly. He lifted a foot from the sand then another, something shiny around his ankle. I couldn't see it well but heard him laugh.

"We got it!" he screamed and slid down the sand hill, a shiny metal crown adorned in jewels in his hand, held high in the air.

"We got it!" I wrapped my arms around him and pressed my lips to his. He returned the kiss before pulling away.

"Not bad for a sylph, right?"

"I didn't say that." Sylph was the true name for air or sky fae but nobody called them that anymore.

He responded, taking a step away, "You didn't have to. That's what you're thinking. What you've been thinking."

I didn't know where he got that from. I hadn't said it. I closed the distance between us that he created. "No. Where is that coming from?"

He tossed the crown my way as I approached. "You know sylph didn't always carry a negative connotation."

I caught the crown with both hands. It was heavy, heavier than I expected. Much heavier than mine. "Tell me?" His hand touched my neck, his fingers rubbed gently under my hair. It felt good. I leaned my neck a little.

"King Syntor and Queen Dafna ruled the fae with honor and love. It was the most peaceful time in ancient fae history. It wasn't until their son Malcurio became king that relations between the fae and others soured."

Every fae knew the story. It was forbidden love. He was common fae and she was royalty, but when he saved the queen's life he was elevated to hero overnight and wed Dafna, the love of his life. They were the ultimate fae power couple but their son, Malcurio, destroyed everything his parents built. It was the sea fae who finally overthrew the crown and took over the throne. The sylphs were never trusted again and the word sylph carried a derogatory tone. It was centuries later that the crown landed in the hands of the land fae, where it remained.

He took the crown from my hands and placed it on my head. "The Diama and the sylph." His fingers moved down my cheeks as his lavender eyes met mine. His soft lips brushed over mine as he pressed them into a kiss. I didn't stop him, didn't want to. His tongue tasted and felt good in my mouth as we stood there beneath the decrepit palace. A breeze sweeping over us and the rhythmic lull of the tides feeding our passion.

When our lips parted, I couldn't help the smile on my face. "Don't get ahead of yourself," I said in jest. "Where next?" I asked, completely energized and ready for the next treasure.

"It says, in the lower dungeon beneath the white palace, a place carved out by impact, you must collect burned and charred sand from the walls and impression of the great tree."

I wrinkled my nose. "What? Lower dungeon." I glanced at the book and held it towards me. There wasn't a picture, only words. "There's a dungeon that was used in ancient times to house prisoners but I've never heard of a lower dungeon and I grew up there. I should know if it exists."

"Did you know the dryad or dark nymphs existed?"

"No."

Soul Fire

"There are many mysteries of our realm."

His words rang with truth. The history of the fae carried ample ambiguities. "OK, but how do we get to it? I can't waltz in looking like this, and the door to the dungeon is guarded. Nobody goes down there. It would turn heads if I did."

A mischievous smile played on his lips. "You're a unicorn. You don't have to go in. Portal me with your horn." He paused and took in my pained expression. "You know how to portal, right?"

"Yes. It's just…nothing… it's a brilliant idea." Sure, I could portal, but I wanted off this wreck of an island.

"That's it then. I'm going to take you some place safe where you can rest."

I climbed on his back as we took off over the seas again. No idea where we were headed, but I trusted him with my life. He'd come through time and time again. My loathing for him softening. The gags he played weren't harmful. They were…well…him.

The flight was short as we landed in a neighborhood, outside a plain house. It was small, like the homes in Provence City. A couple trees in the front yard and a walkway of Navarin flowers. I didn't know much about plants or their names but the trees were common to the realm, with large oval leaves, and the flowers bloomed in various colors. They, too, were common.

"C'mon. This is my house."

When I didn't follow, he paused. "What? Too good for a common home?"

I shook my head. "What about your parents? The Diama can't go into their house looking like this. I'm not presentable."

He rolled his eyes. "No lights. They aren't home."

Most of the other homes did have some type of light. "Fine."

The home inside was cozy. The walls light-yellow color and a few family pictures hung from them. In the middle of the house was a large room with doors to all the other rooms and a short hallway. I followed him down the short hallway that led to a restroom and another room with a closed door. He opened the door. "This is my room. You can stay here."

The rest of the home was neat and tidy but his room was a disaster. Clothes hung from his bed and piled on the smooth wood flooring, along with a scattering of books and clothes pushed under his bed. The top drawer of a bureau hung open with a shirt dangling over the edge.

He responded to the grimace marring my face. "We leave my door closed. I'm not here much so it gets messy and my parents refuse to clean it when I'm at the academy."

Soul Fire

I didn't want to sound rude and it was just clothes and books. Not creepy crawlies like the mangroves. "Its fine. Not as bad as other places we've been today."

He emptied his pocket, pulling out the dryad leaf and Ansley's bottle of dust and laid them on the top of his bureau. Grabbing a small empty tube, he stuffed it in his pocket. "But not fit for a Diama." The sadness in his words stabbed like a sword.

"Let's do this. Turn around. Once I transform, I'll portal you behind the dungeon doors. You'll have to find the lower dungeon on your own. I don't know where it is."

He turned around and I transformed. The room seemed smaller because I was bigger, but still small for a unicorn. He turned around and faced me.

I pointed my horn towards him and thought of the dungeon. I'd only seen it once. With it in mind, I sent a ripple of energy through my horn. A violet light swallowed him in a matter of seconds and I was alone.

9

Bjorn

The violet light dissolved and left me in the darkness. Snapping my fingers, I said 'Illumi' and a sconce on the wall lit up. I was at the bottom of the stairs. At the top of them were two thick, tall, double doors. The guards stood on the other side of those. Ahead of me was a hallway. It was the only path.

Following it, the sconce lit ahead of me and darkened behind me. The walls of the dungeon were rough, hardened sand bricks. An archway ahead led to a chamber to the right and to the left. The chambers had their own doors. I didn't open them but opened the book. When I found the page, a wind swept behind me, pushing me into the air and through the hallway then down, down, down and finally landed me on my feet in front of a massive door.

My eyes followed the height of the door then the width. Glancing at the book, the door I stood before showed a hand. It drew two interlocking arrow heads and words in old fae appeared below. *Enter to find, the secrets of time.*

I drew the arrows on the door and repeated the words. The door creaked and moaned. Slowly, it opened. A light shimmered in the middle then brightened, displaying the entire room. It was nothing more than a large cavern with paintings covering the walls and the smell was moldier than the higher dungeons. The odor mingled with sea water. I wished I had a shirt on to cover my nose.

Studying the pictures, they were scenes; colorful but not all fae. A man with a staff, a golden stone in the handle, lowered it to the ground and the pictures moved. I stepped back and watched. A golden light spread over the ground and plants and life emerged. All the paintings coming to life, then darkness overcame the population, heads turned and the sky and the room went black.

Light twinkled from the center of the room and spread slowly outward at a level plane like a disk. On the other side of the room was a tree. It wasn't colorful but dark as if burned into the wall. The book said: *a place carved out by impact you must collect burned and charred sand from the walls and impression of the great tree.* The saying that opened the door said: *enter to find, secrets of time.* My mouth dropped open as I realized what I was seeing. It didn't seem a hybrid ice dragon/ sylph like me had any business with the secrets of time and life.

The staff and the golden stone wasn't a stone at all but a seed from the Serenity Tree in Aradia, the elfin realm. Life sprung from it, covering the realms, and the tree grew. I couldn't believe I was witness to this. Getting hold of myself, I moved to the tree and brushed it with my finger. Soot dropped. I pulled the glass tube from my pocket and collected enough soot to fill it.

It was done. Now I had to find a way out. An ethereal female voice spoke: *Go up the stairs and find the back door. When you touch it, it will unlock.*

The heavy door closed behind me as the light dimmed. The wall sconces lit and unlit as I walked past them up the stairs. A door suddenly appeared. I hadn't remembered seeing it but I was carried on a wind and probably missed it. Touching the door, it opened into the night. There were no guards. As the door closed, it blended into the wall as if it was never there.

The most likely explanation was magic. I ran over the beach and spread my wings into the air. Lifting myself high over the sea, I did a couple spins in the air in celebration, anxious to get back to the spoiled Diama who was growing on me. *I did it!* What was next I hadn't checked. My hope was Halsey hadn't freaked in my absence.

10

Halsey

I wrapped my arms around Bjorn as he held up the small tube filled with black dust. A smug smile on his face. "You did it! You got it!"

He lifted me into the air, his hands around my waist, and spun. "We did it!" He lowered me slowly to the ground and handed me the book. "What's next?"

Words scrolled over the page. Place the crown in a cauldron with the charred remains of the tree and the dryad's leaf, sprinkle Ansley's dust over it and repeat the words: *violence, death, life and love, show me the footsteps to the grimoire's dove.*

Soul Fire

Dove. What was a dove? We looked at each other with puzzled expressions.

"Where do we find a cauldron?" he asked.

That was his question. I glanced again and reread the words. It didn't say it had to be a specific cauldron. His weirdness had really grown on me. "Provence Academy of course!"

He scratched his head. "I knew that."

Provence City was quiet as we entered through the curtain from Navarin. It was a small, circular place, carved from each realm, but had its own distinguishing characteristics so it would be a safe place for all subspecies to coexist. It housed the academy and Provence Hall, where the tribunal met. A council of representatives from all the realms. We stayed on the path beneath silver and purple-leafed trees and came around the back of the academy past the courtyard that led to the cafeteria. We'd have to go through the front door to get to the classrooms.

Bjorn lowered himself to a squat behind a bush and waved me to join him. "We go in through the gym. It'll draw less attention. We grab the cauldron and head back to Navarin."

Why? The directions didn't specify a certain cauldron or location. "Why don't we just do the spell here?"

REALM WALKER

He pinched his lips and shrugged as his eyes scanned the directions in the book. "Alright."

I followed behind him as we neared the back door by the gym. He sprinkled dust, drew on the lock, and said 'druppo' – the old fae word we used to unlock doors. It was a simple sigil and wouldn't work on doors spelled with heavy magic, but in Provence that wasn't a problem since nothing higher than level 2 magic could be used.

The door clicked and he wrapped his hands around the infinity door handle and pushed. The gym looked different at night, without any lights, but from the open door on the other side enough dim light spread from the hallway for us to see. He reached his hand behind him, I took it and we walked through the gym.

He peeked around the corner then slipped into the hallway. I stayed behind him, my hand in his as we reached the floating staircase that would take us to the second floor. My leg brushed one of the large brass posts of the baluster and I pressed my vacant hand to the gem-studded banister. The cerulean flowers closed at night. In the day, they opened and hung upside down. They were called eternal tear drops because they looked like tear drops.

The academy was eerily silent at night, almost morning now. It wouldn't be long before sunrise and we needed to be done before that. He pushed the door open to Midge's classroom. She was our instructor who taught fae spells that required cauldrons. They were heavier spells than simple sigils.

We placed the crown, leaf, and ash from the dungeon in the cauldron on the table in the middle of the room. Bjorn opened the small bottle of Ansley's dust and dropped some into my hand then his. My stomach did flip flops and I sucked in a deep breath to calm my nerves. Pinching the dust in my fingers I sprinkled it over the items in unison with Bjorn. We chanted, "violence, death, life and love, show me the footsteps to the grimoire's dove."

The items lit up and swirled then lifted out of the cauldron, forming the shape of a man, glittering in Ansley's dust. I glanced down, my eyes in disbelief as the cauldron was empty. From the corner of my eye the book broke into tiny pieces of dust that swirled into a ball and vanished with a flash of light. I'd pulled a Terra on Terra and borrowed the book without Terra's knowledge, I'd replace it with a fake.

Without time to ponder it, the fairy dust form walked out of the room and down the stairs. We followed behind. He walked right out the front door and around the large school towards Navarin.

REALM WALKER

Neither of us said a word as we followed him back through the curtain to Navarin. He walked through the green sand and over the lavender sea. Bjorn followed him through the air as we glided above him, staying low until we reached the island of the white palace. He walked right through a statue of the first land fae queen then vanished.

Bjorn skidded to a stop and we both stared at the statue in disbelief. White wings formed behind it. They flapped and moved upwards. Reaching above the statue's head, a white bird appeared. In its mouth was a scroll. It fluttered in front of us. I put out my hands and it dropped it into them then disappeared into the statue.

I blinked my eyes in awe, I swallowed and dropped my eyes to the scroll in my hands. A wax seal with an M in the center. "This is it!"

"The most powerful spell among the realms. One that requires sacrifice…" Bjorn's voice fell off. His Adam's apple bobbed as he swallowed, our eyes met, and a joyful smile spread over his face. "We actually did it! I didn't even think this thing actually existed when we started out but it... it does!"

My lips matched his smile. "We did. We did it! Together!" I jumped in excitement and pressed my lips to his. His arms snaked behind my lower back, his hand moving below my waist as I wrapped mine over his back, accepting all he gave me. The sun rose around us as the new day began.

Epilogue

Halsey

After class, I climbed the staircase. Hearing Terra was back, I hoped to catch her in the room. Opening the door, I quickly diverted my eyes and strode past Terra to my closet. A baggy T-shirt hung over her shoulders, covering to her knees.

My lips pulled upward in a beaming smile I didn't want her to see. It would give her too much pleasure and she'd know immediately I'd done something to help her. I couldn't give her that pleasure yet. Our relationship wasn't one of love or trust, but we had an understanding. "How was Lols?" Otherwise known as the Land of Lost Souls, where she and her closest friends had been sent. Her absence gave me the opportunity.

"Home. I miss it," she responded, as if not wanting to be bothered.

I found the legendary grimoire that was more of an urban myth. No one knew it really existed, especially after so many centuries had passed. I pushed the clothes in my closet and pulled the scroll from the coat pocket I'd hidden it in. In my hands was the most powerful spell of all time and Bjorn and I found it without Terra's help. Keeping my back to Terra to hide my widening smile, I responded, "Oh."

"What is it?" Terra asked, her tone giving away her curiosity.

Pulling my lips down, I tried to hide my pride. I'd beaten Terra and Merla, the most powerful fae of all time. *Beat* was a strong word. I did something Merla never expected. That's why she'd hidden the clues in a book and Terra was always one-upping me. It was my turn. I spun around, fighting my smile that wouldn't stop, keeping the scroll behind my back. Her colorful eyes searched my arms.

"What?" Terra said, sharper than she expected.

I brought my hands forward, unable to contain myself. "I got it!" I said, holding the scroll in front of her.

Her face said a million words; expectation, shock, joy, "How did you?"

My inner mischievous self giggled as I bold-face lied to her. It wasn't like she hadn't manipulated me many times. "The other book was a map. I know I shouldn't have, but don't be mad. I found it in your closet and returned it once I translated it then went to Navarin and followed the map."

Terra's lips pushed together and her eyes narrowed as she studied my face. As if she was calculating whether I was being honest or not. "Who helped you?"

"Bjorn." An awkward silence filled the room and I shifted nervously. "He's not that bad."

When realization hit Terra, she sat on the edge of her bed, her eyes widened into spheres and her mouth formed a large circle. "Ohh, you and Bjorn."

I played with my hands nervously and brushed off Terra's shock. "It's nothing. I'm the Diama. We had fun."

I pushed her shock off, flipped my full hair, and dropped the scroll into her lap. She smoothed her hand over it and studied the seal. She understood the gravity of the object in her hand.

My job was done. I'd finally gotten the best of my roommate and now I had other things to do, like meet Bjorn.

Soul Fire

He sat on the edge of the stone ledge of the veranda in front of the school, his glider propped against the side. Seeing me, he rose, a cunning smile playing on his lips. I folded my arms around his neck. "What mischievousness is your brain plotting?"

A lick of his bottom lip and a glint in his eye, he responded, "None." His freckles bouncing with the word as his lips met mine.

He pulled away, the silly smile still on his face and slid an arm from around my waist and collected his glider. "I can't fly in Provence, but I can show you the next best thing."

He dropped his glider when he reached the bottom step. It hovered over the ground. I stepped on after him, one foot in front of the other, as the board was slender. My arms around his waist as we zipped into the woods.

Realm Walker

Accidental Ghost
Soul Catcher Vol. 1

1

Halloween came every day for me since I fell into a river of blood in a realm I'd never heard of. It was innocent. I was spelunking when I dropped through a cavern and into Blood River. Terra a hybrid saved me. She even got me back home after I was kidnapped by vampires and escaped to Thraves, land of the harvesters where I met death and learned my destiny. Sometimes I'd give my soul to return to my former life.

I dropped the pickaxe. I wouldn't get the hang of it. The pick wasn't working for me.

I glanced at my trainer in his spirit form.

"I'll never get it right."

"You will."

"I'm your punishment, aren't I?" He was a prominent tribunal representative for the Harvester realm of Thraves before I dropped into his realm spelunking.

"No. My punishment is being kicked off the tribunal because of my own actions."

There were eight realms all of them represented on the tribunal except the human realm or Lols for Land of Lost souls. They called us commoners. We were anything but common and I resented being called common.

"We'll try again tomorrow."

"Sure," I climbed the steps to the brownstone. He vanished into the night. His spirit returning to Thraves. Harvesters could only harvest souls in Lols in spirit form. I had a beef with this realm being called that. Souls here weren't lost we were home on Earth or wherever it was. As a harvester hybrid I could harvest in my physical form.

I rolled the rocks from each realm between my fingers. I was a hybrid of five realms; Verboten, Aradia, Sier, Canida and Thraves meaning I was a troll, elf, dragon,

Soul Fire

Lycan and harvester hybrid. According to death I not only had to collect a rock from each realm but had to enter it which I had. I didn't know what good the Drakonian rock did since I wasn't vampire but death insisted it was useful. She was cryptic.

I bore the mark of each realm on my chest. A passport that allowed me to enter and exit any realm I was part of.

Harvesting wasn't a perfect science and Metford, my instructor and were learning together. Evidently harvester hybrids weren't common.

That was six months ago. I had improved in the art of harvesting but still had some troubles.

The dark soul latched onto my pickaxe and wouldn't let go. I hit the end on the ground, hoping to jar it lose but it clung like sticky goo.

"Easy, don't let frustration get you."

Easy for him to say. Metford was born in Thraves and designed for harvesting. I held the pickaxe upward like he'd taught me, the black ball rose finally. It was ascending to the otherworld. The place dark souls go.

No, no, no I screamed in my head as a tiny piece of it stuck. It looked like a black blob of stretched slime. The yellow stone in the eye of the pickaxe flashed.

One of the rocks used to trap the souls was blinking in and out. When a soul was trapped, they shone bright, connecting in a six-point star. I kept the pickaxe steady as I maneuvered myself to the rock then carefully lowered myself.

I kept the pickaxe stable as I could with one hand, lowered myself and touched the rock. Its energy returned and the pesky dark soul continued its ascension as the tiny stuck piece became unstuck.

I dropped the axe and sighed.

"You're improving," Metford said in a congratulatory tone.

I held up my hand to high five but his spirit hand went right through mine.

2

My eyelids drooped as I worked to keep them open. Taking another gulp of my double shot iced coffee wasn't enough. Harvesting and early morning classes didn't work but it was the only time this class was offered.

Dr. Blyzbub took her glasses off, twirling them in her hand as she spoke. "Vickery House in upstate New York is an example of spirit attachment to a structure. Several families moved in and were scared out after complaints of paranormal events. The families all lived ghost free lives after leaving.

It has been said the house could be a gateway between the living and the dead. The house has been unoccupied since 1947."

Thanks to being a harvester, I now had a double major; paranormal studies and geology which meant sleepless nights for the next three years. Adding paranormal studies meant more classes. Therefore, I take a class at eight in the morning instead of sleeping. Dr. Blyzbub was full of stories of hauntings. This weekend I'd check out Vickery House.

I searched it on my laptop and saved the address. It was in the town of Blake. A small quintessential town with cobblestone streets and mom and pop locally owned shops.

Vickery House put it on the map. They don't do tours in the house but it is part of a tour of Blake.

I stuffed my laptop into my bag and pulled it over my shoulder. It was time to go home and sleep before tonight's harvesting.

"How about a coffee?" Sharae asked.

She was hot, sweet and had been flirting with me since the beginning of the semester but I didn't have time to date and I had a thing for a girl I hadn't seen in months – Terra.

The girl who saved me in Drakonia. What we had was an attraction and hadn't gone beyond a couple kisses but I couldn't get her out of my mind.

Soul Fire

Our destinies weren't intertwined. I was stuck here harvesting and she was saving the realms.

It was time to move on but not today. My bed was calling. "Thanks but not today. I had a late night," her face dropped as the words left my mouth. I'd turned her down so many times.

Her deep brown eyes turned downward, "sure, another time."

I felt like roadkill driven over by many cars.

I liked her. What wasn't to like. She had the right size curves, a sweet smile, a caramel complexion, endless brown eyes and was interested in the dead.

My alarm went off, it's annoying ring blasting in my ear. I chose it so I'd wake up. Rings that weren't obnoxious became part of my dreams and I slept through them.

I slid the ringer off instead of snooze and got up. My stomach complaining about being empty. A side-effect of being a full-time student with a double major and moonlighting as a harvester was never having time to shop or do laundry. I pulled on a pair of sweats that smelled freshish and slipped on a pair of shoes.

The beauty of living in New York was food was always close.

I picked up all the clothes on my floor and tossed them into a bag with soap pods and dryer sheets. There was a laundromat on the corner before the coffee shop.

After tossing my clothes in the machine I walked next door and ordered a ham and cheese croissant and double shot iced coffee.

I turned on my computer and continued my research of Vickery House.

It seemed a pretty typical haunting, an unrested dark soul. Noises like scraping against the floor and even in the heat of the summer a specific room was chilly.

Wait, maybe not so typical. A young couple bought the house in the spring of 1946. His niece came to live with them after her mother died. Soon she started talking to herself, carrying on conversations that escalated into her sleepwalking and eventually the girl refused to go back into the house. She interacted with the spirit. Maybe she was a harvester hybrid too. She went home to her father but the nonsense didn't stop and eventually she killed herself.

Spirits of unrest generally went about their business the day they died, repeating it day after day. This one hadn't.

No one ever died in the house but its occupants always complained of the same things, strange noises and a freezing room. Of course anyone who ever lived in the house was dead and no one ever died in the house.

Soul Fire

I finished my clothes, returned to my brownstone and showered.

Metford's voice entered my head from the comicay, a gel device that fit above the wrist. The harvesters gave it to me. It was used for communication among other things.

Our meeting place tonight was the Midnight Sugar Company in Dublin Ohio.

The elevators or gateways made it much easier to travel the land of the living and get there quickly. They were a static disturbance, found often times in cemeteries but not always. As a harvester who saw spirits the ones in cemeteries were the easiest for me to find. They allowed me travel anywhere in Lols. I stepped in and thought of where I was going. The elevator vanished as I stood on the sidewalk outside the candy store. A large sign was outside the storefront. On either side of two lollipops were the words Dublin Ohio. Beneath that Midnight est. 1952 and beneath that Sugar Company.

Did someone fall into a vat of chocolate and drown or eat too much taffy?

Metford appeared at my side. He was tall and thick with a goatee he was always tugging at as I was in the middle of harvesting. It was a nervous habit and lately he didn't tug so much. I was getting better.

"A honeymooning couple died in the hotel across the street in 1993. It was a double homicide, and the killer was never apprehended."

I never asked where he got his info. My eyes swept the hotel. It was several stories high.

"It was in rm. 513."

Great. Metford stayed at my side filling me in on the details of the couple's death as I strolled into the hotel.

Situated on the left was a large circular check in counter. To the right were plush sage colored couches and chairs and wooden tables. A large mural of a river and woods in a modern style was painted on one wall.

The clerk at the counter smiled as I walked past him as if I was a guest returning from dinner. No one but me could see Metford as he was in spirit form. Sometimes I forgot and talked back to him. I got strange looks when that happened.

I pressed the button and waited as the elevator descended and the doors opened.

I didn't really have a plan but was hoping the room would be empty.

I knocked on 513 and didn't get an answer. That was good. I slid the stone from Sier over the card pad and the door unlocked. Each stone did its own special thing.

Once inside I dropped my harvester bag onto the bed. It was a Coach I found at the secondhand shop. I guessed its previous owner got rid of it for the next years style. It worked. I looked inconspicuous and the pickaxe fit into it nicely without catching any eyes.

I placed the rocks at equal points in the middle of the room after rubbing them together in my hands. The process recharged them. I grabbed the pickaxe and waited.

The couple had returned about nine according to the night clerk. Their screams were heard about an hour later. It was 8:56.

At 9:07 the couple came in kissing. Their hands all over each other. Clothes dropped to the floor and I turned. They were dead but it still felt an invasion of their privacy. Not really a horrible thing to make love every day before dying. I'd seen worse in my six months of harvesting.

I let the rocks do their thing as the couple's spirits coalesced into the center of the rocks.

I touched the female as she was closest. Her soul shining white on the pick. I brought it upward and watched as her spirit ascended. I then touched the man's soul, also white, both pure souls, and raised it.

The door opened. Fudge! I looked to Metford like he could help but as a spirit there was nothing he could do.

The man's spirit ascended. It would have been an easy job. Pure souls usually were.

Realm Walker

A tall man stared at me, his mouth gaping. I guessed he'd never seen a 19-year-old with a pickaxe in a hotel. He looked like a businessman with his expensive suit, short, combed back wavy hair and clean-shaven face. By his unsteady gait it appeared he'd had a few too many to drink as he stumbled towards me and fell.

I tried to slip out of the way but couldn't in time as his shoulder dropped into my arm that held the pickaxe.

In a panic I flipped him over with my free hand and sighed relief when it had only grazed him. Dribbles of blood bubbled around the wound.

"Leave him." Metford said, tugging his goatee so hard I thought he'd pull it out.

"I can't. He's hurt."

"You're here to harvest souls. He'll heal from the injury."

Sure he would but I couldn't leave him like that. I ran to the bathroom and wet a washcloth and pressed it against his arm until the bleeding stopped.

Metford grumbled something as I rummaged around the man's cosmetic bag in search of bandages.

At the bottom of the bag and looking as if they'd been in the bag for years. The wrappers discolored and wrinkled were two regular size adhesive bandages. I ripped the wrappers off and pressed them over the wound.

"Since you interfered and shouldn't have, don't leave anything at the scene." Metford scolded.

I wore gloves, always. They were part of my kit. I lashed back at him, "What if he had died? How can you be so cold?"

I collected the rocks and put them back into the velvet bag I kept them in then the pickaxe and last I rolled up the bloody washcloth and tossed it in the bag.

"I'm not uncaring," Metford claimed as if trying to convince himself.

"What would I have done if he'd died besides harvest his soul?"

"That didn't happen."

"But what if it had?" I imagined myself with a murder rap. I'd be guilty with no excuse. I was sure harvesting souls wouldn't count as an excuse for an accidental murder. I'd be laughed out of court and sentenced, or I'd have to plea.